Her First Taste: Volume One

By
Khalani Jones

DEDICATION

This book is dedicated to all who have ever loved

the taste of a woman.

CONTENTS

ACKNOWLEDGMENTS

Thank you to all the muses known and unknown
who

 made this work possible. The following is a
collection

of thoughts, fantasy, and reality blended together.

What follows is a peak into my mind.

I hope each page leaves you sensually satisfied.

The Coffee Shop: Carmel Delight Edition

Part One

From the moment I walked into the coffee shop I felt her eyes on me. I felt she was sitting on the left side by the entrance, as if she were waiting on something. Feeling like playing a game of cat and mouse I decided to play along and sit directly on the other side of the room, allowing her full access to stare as she pleased.   "Hi, Can I help you." The waitress' voice knocked me out of my thoughts and back to reality. "Oh, yes sorry. I was just distracted." I paused as I looked the waitress up and down and noticed she was a beauty in herself. Full figured, mocha smooth skin, and dreads pulled into a ponytail. "I would like an iced coffee."

"With or without whip cream," she said in a slow seductive tone. I watched her lick her lips while she waited on my response. "With whip cream," I paused, "it's sweeter that way," I smiled. "I'll put that right in for you." She walked away swinging her hips, putting on a show for me. I shook my head and made a mental note to leave my card with her.

I had almost forgotten about the pair of staring eyes from across the room. When I looked up and didn't see her I was a bit disappointed. She could have been fun I thought. I looked down at my phone when I could sense someone standing in front of me.

"Excuse me is someone sitting here?" "No, take a seat," I said straightening up my stance. I was careful not to smirk now that the pair of eyes were in front of me, yet I was eager to match a personality with the boldness of her stares. "What took you so long to approach I was starting to think you weren't interested." "Well I had to wait for that waitress to finish throwing herself at you." Observant and feisty I like it I thought.

At this moment, the waitress returned with my coffee. I could see on her face she was disappointed that I now had company. Not to tie myself to this stranger, I offered her my card and told her to contact me when she could. Watching her face light up warmed my heart. I loved working out and staying fit, but I liked my women to have curves to hold. I had been dating too many gym rats lately and though the sex was good, sometimes you just wanted a meal without calculating how many calories it had and how long we would have to stay in the gym to burn it off. I sipped my coffee, enjoying the silence.

"So how long have you and your boyfriend been together?" She looked up surprised and coughed, chocking on her iced latté. "What? I don't." I put my hand up. "Don't lie to me. I felt from the moment I walked in. You want something I could give you. But, you are conflicted because you have a commitment. Which is another reason it took you so long to approach. And based on your presence in front of me it's a commitment that is boring you. So tell me how long you have been together and when is the last time you were satisfied. I can help you with the last one, but I should tell you now I don't wreck homes. I just enjoy," I paused ", pleasing women. "

She still looked like a deer caught in headlights. I realized maybe I had come a bit too direct at her. "Look I'm sorry, I'm just a straight forward person. I've been lied to by plenty of straight women who I thought were wifey material but I was just their jump-off. So excuse my aggressiveness. It's just rare that someone approaches me on some I want to get to know you for you type of thing."   "Three years. You're right about all of what you said that surprises me. You read people very well." "If you get hurt enough it's a skill you pick up," I replied. "He hasn't satisfied me in about a year and a half. Every time we have sex I pretend to orgasm really quickly, but in reality after he goes to sleep I touch myself until I'm pleased. And he never knows." I made a mental note that not only was this woman observant, she was also deceptive. I would have to be careful.   "So why are you still with him?" "Finances, it's just easier to stay together. We are set to get married in the fall. But before I take that plunge I just needed to know what it was like to…" She trailed off and I finished her sentence. "Be with a woman."   My phone dinged alerting me that my coffee break was over. It was time to go back to the hospital. "Look one time that's all I can offer you," I said. "Here is my card call me when you're ready. I didn't get your name by the way." "Amanda." 'I look forward to hearing from you Amanda," I smiled as I walked away wondering when I was going to settle down with a nice woman, someone to introduce to the family. Ding, a text "Mariah, I enjoyed last night." I replied, "me too, let's do it again tonight." I shook my head at myself and realized that if I wanted wifey material I was going to have to switch my game up. I was having too much fun and not enough seriousness. I would put an effort in, I decided, after my escapades with Ms. Amanda.

The Coffee Shop: Carmel Delight Edition

Part Two

The next morning, I woke up with a text from Amanda. "So when are we going to do this?" I looked at the text and almost deleted it before I remembered that she was going to be my last bit of fun before I settled down and started to look for someone to build something with. "What's something you want at this little party?" As soon as I had sent it I got a text back that said "Handcuffs." I smiled, so far Amanda had three things working for her: she was sexy, she was to the point, and she was kinky. The rest of the morning I let Amanda's text go un-responded until lunch when I hit her back with a text that said "Meet me at my house on 9 p.m. on Saturday." It was 7 on Saturday evening when I went down my checklist for the evening with

Amanda: Blindfolds, handcuffs, ice bucket, whipped cream, caramel. Check, check and double check I thought. I walked around nervously straightening the already clean house when I chuckled. I couldn't believe I was nervous for Amanda to arrive at my townhome. While I couldn't put my finger on it, I was unusually excited and decided to mentally plan how the night would go. I planned a candle light dinner followed by a back massage in dim lights. Then, we would progress to my Fuck Room equipped with an assortment of various sized straps, flavored sexual enhancers, and warming massage oils. I hoped she was into rough play because I also has a pair of nipple clamps, silk ties, whips, and more. I could feel my clit

14

swelling as I thought about her moans muffled by her face in my pillow. I slipped my hand between my thighs rocking back and forth, biting my lip from how wet I was. "Ding, Dong" The doorbell ringing interrupted my impromptu masturbation session. I thought about finishing the deed, but decided to wait for the real thing.

I glanced at my watch, 8:55. I love an early woman, I smiled. I opened the door greeted by a warm Atlanta night with a cool breeze and Amanda in a trench coat. I chuckled, she is not playing I thought. "You're early," I said. "On the contrary, I'm right on time," she said. Upon entering the house, she handed me the belt that was holding her coat closed. As she handed me the belt I noticed a set of perky nipples peeking out from under her coat. My mouth watered. "How'd you get out of house with that on? Your man didn't have any questions." I told you there is no passion in our relationship. I could walk out of that apartment naked and he would never know." "That's a shame," I said as I pulled her into my arms. I wiped a tear from her eye. "Well for tonight I am going to let you know what it feels like for someone to notice all of you." She wrapped her legs around me and we kissed like we had known each other for longer than we had. Our tongues danced around each other gently, then with intensifying force. I pulled away first. She took her hand traced my jar and pulled me towards her again as if my touch was healing her in some way like she needed my lips to try to convey the feelings she couldn't use words to say. At that moment, I decided to skip dinner and instead took her hand and lead her up the stairs to my Fuck Room. The mood was set for an evening of pain and pleasure. Candles in all four corners of the rooms illuminated it in a calming glow. The scent from the candles was serving as aroma therapy. And there in the middle of the bed was a pair of pink lace handcuffs. She walked up to the bed turned around and smiled and said "you remembered." "I never forget anything a lady tells me, "I replied.   I walked over to her slowly and whispered in her ear ", lay down." While she slowly laid across the bed I admired her curves from behind. I grabbed the massage oil and warmed it in my hands. I stared at her shoulders paying attention to the tension around her neck. I could hear her breathing become shallow. I smirked because I knew we had barely begun. I took the oil and dripped it down her back watching her back arch from the coolness of it against her skin. Using my right hand, I traced the line of oil down the middle of her back and used my left hand to cup her ass. Squeezing it gently I then took my right hand and used it to part her legs.   Kissing her shoulders and knowing she was completely relaxed I took the blindfold and tied it around her eyes. She raised her head up. I pushed her shoulders back down and said, "trust me." I began to kiss every inch of her body.   First, her left shoulder blade then the right, down to the small of her back to her ass cheeks, down her right leg and up the left one. By this time, I knew she was beyond ready for whatever was about to happen next. I reached over to the side of the bed and grabbed a piece of ice from the ice bucket.   "Turn over," I commanded her. While she was still blindfolded I took the ice in my mouth and began to suck on it gently just to get it to begin to melt. Then I placed it on her collar bone. She receded in shock.   I trailed the ice down to her nipples watching as they became harder with each touch of the ice. The first piece melted.

I grabbed another piece repeated the same process, but this time I started rubbing the ice across her stomach and further down to the place where her thighs ended and her pussy began. Now I could hear her moaning, see her pelvis grinding in anticipation.

The Coffee Shop: Carmel Delight Edition

Part Three

With the small tip of ice that was left I guided it into her pussy. I watched her reaction as her body went from shock to ecstasy. I laughed knowing that we hadn't even fucked yet and I had made her cum more than her man had in the last year and a half. I took my hand and guided two fingers into her. I was greeted by wet walls and moans. "Mariah." Usually during sex, I didn't like to hear my name called, but tonight it was turning me on. I pushed my fingers deeper, pushed her legs up higher until I could feel her dripping down my arm. "Shit. I pulled my fingers out and slowly slid them back in her pussy inch by inch. I felt her tightening her lips around me and grinding into my hands. As her orgasm took over I felt her scratching her nails into my back deeper and deeper. But before she could climax again I and got up to grab my strap and the handcuffs.   I took her arms and lightly handcuffed them behind her back. She was still blindfolded so she couldn't see me. I laid her onto her back and grabbed the caramel, spreading it across her abs. I slowly licked it off knowing I was teasing her.   Her moans intensified as my tongue dipped in and out of her belly button. If she was out of the cuffs I knew she would have had her hands in my dreads. Just the thought of her hands playing in my hair got me even more excited.   Then, I got the bottle of whip cream and sprayed it on her flowing mound. Slowly, I slid the strap into her. She gasped not expecting to be penetrated so easily. The deeper I went, the more I knew she wanted to dig her nails in my back, but she couldn't because of the handcuffs so she clinched her legs around me as tight as she could. The more she called out my name the more I wanted to keep fucking her. But I could only tease a beautiful woman so long before I had to let go. I pulled out and grabbed the key to un-do her handcuffs.   I fucked her furiously falling in love with the sounds of my thighs against her wet ass pussy. As I came I grabbed her hips drilling the strap into her as I dripped down her legs. I felt sweat drip from my forehead while I caught my breath.   I picked her up and laid her back against the wall. I slowly twisted my hips back and forth getting lost in the feel of her body. I kissed her neck and squeezed her nipples which were hard as rocks. My fingers found her clit and slowly rubbed it while her breaths got shorter. I suddenly felt overrun with emotion and slowly pulled the strap out.

"Did you enjoy my version of caramel delight," I asked. She smiled and reached over to kiss me. We stayed in that position all night. When she finally fell asleep I found myself dreading the fact that not only was she leaving my house in a few hours she was going back to her man. I rolled over and kissed her cheek, knowing that the moment was bitter sweet, knowing I needed more.

The Writers: Part One

If it was anything I loved in this world more than writing it was sex. I loved how sensual it could be, how animalistic it could be, how spiritual it could be, and most of all how fucking good it could feel. So it goes without saying I was looking forward to my mandatory writing session with my Literature classmates. After all, I had luckily been assigned one of my crushes to work with. The only negative was that I had to share my journal with her. I wonder would she judge what I wrote? Would she be able to recognize the poems about her? Worst of all, would she think I was some sort of sex feign? I looked over my latest piece which I titled "The Re-Twist"

The Re-Twist

Your hands check out the scene
Tug them,
Pull them apart
Feel the tension as they part-
Easily
Greasily
Put some on your fingers and as I scream
Be gentle apologize.
Tell me it's almost over
Pull my head closer
Twist and turn over and over...
Round one done
Admiring these new parts like light in a cloister.

I hoped that by reading it she recognized the

juxtaposition between hair and sexuality. I

hoped she got it, that she understood me. I

shook my feelings of doubt and rushed to our

Starbucks meeting.

Soon as I arrived the smell of coffee engulfed me. For some reason the scene felt slightly euphoric, I sat down with a Frappuccino as my chosen aphrodisiac and waited for Lani to arrive. I checked my phone, I had misread her message. We were supposed to meet at 3:15 not 3. With the extra time, I decided to write a poem I called "Ode to Usher."

Ode to Usher
Could you handle it
If I told you how I really feel
Infiltrated your mind first
Just so I could make sure these feelings are real
So can I go there to that forbidden place
Do I have your permission to get lost in your waist?
Hope all this time hasn't been a waste
Every time I think about you a smile cascades my face
Wanna let the world know
make you my woman crush everyday of the week

but I don't wanna come off as weak
so tell me
would you could you...
could we?
could we?
Be more than this moment or does this
experience just end?

As I read it back I wiggled in my seat enjoying

the feeling of my clit pressing against my jeans. I

closed my eyes and imagined Lani's lips

pressing against my sacred place. I ground my

hips like she was tasting me. I had wanted her

for so long I could feel my clit pounding. My

nectar spilled from the top to the bottom of my

lips while she kissed my mound. I was close to

erupting and she hadn't even fucked me.

"Sorry for making you wait." I jumped from the sound of her voice interrupting my almost complete fantasy. "It's cool," I slowly replied. As I spoke I took the time to admire her beauty. Brown eyes, curly natural hair, thick thighs to hold onto, and a stomach pouch to kiss, lick, and suck all night. I shook my head, now wasn't a time for fantasy, it was a time for focus.

"Danielle, I'm ready to exchange journals when you are." I shyly closed my journal and handed it to her. While I was still nervous as to what she would think of my work, I was more excited to explore her thoughts.

The first page I tuned to was intriguing.

Contemplations on Life Written When I have a Theology Assignment Due
Does Sexuality lead to sensuality?
More questions- Do I really have individuality?
Do u have to have a spirit for spirituality?
Or are we all pawns in the masses lost in a fallacy?
Try so hard but in actuality...
Nobody knows the difference between the fakeness and reality.

After I read it, I glanced at her. She looked

engrossed in my journal. I shifted my eyes back

to her work. Her writing surprised me, I didn't

know her writing would be so raw or her

thoughts so deep. I could feel my cheeks burning

as my infatuation grew into a full- blown crush. I

smiled as I turned the page to the next piece.

For All the Hoes
You looking for a Boaz
Wit yo hoe azz
Like having sex with every nigga
Is just living free as-
A bird.
And that's your right
so pop that pussy girl
Open them legs up tonight.
And after he bust and leave you for the night
Don't contemplate life
Cuz u a independent woman
And that nigga was just trife.

This piece struck me. Who was she writing about? Her self? Another woman? Someone she doesn't know at all? I made a mental note to ask her more about that piece. My heart started to race at the thought of Lani being sexually intimate with a woman. I didn't know her business, but I just assumed she had a dude dicking her down at night. I wanted to be brave and just ask her if she was into women. But, the thought of her saying no stopped me. My trait as a writer was to observe and let actions speak for themselves. While my logic was usually sound, right now didn't seem like the time to wait for Lani's actions to reveal her sexual preference. I shook my head frustrated at my hesitance. I turned the page to the last piece in her journal.

Untitled

Axioms and maximums
Searching for truth
Within yourself and outside
Which is better for the night?
Meditations to get high
or
Drugs for the release
The battle proceeds
 between the strong and the weak...

Damn her last piece really struck a nerve with me. She liked to meditate? Each thing I learned about her made me want to uncover even more of her mystery. I sat silently while I waited for her to finish going through my journal. When she finished, she looked up and smiled. "Wow Danielle, you're really talented." "I really enjoyed your verb use it's like you pull the reader in." She paused, "I have to admit some of them felt kind of…personal. Like I could picture myself in them." I started to speak, but she held up her hand stopping me mid-breath. "The other thing I enjoyed was the pure sensual nature of your more sexual pieces. The connection between the characters seems spiritual and sexual. Almost Tantric-like, to be honest, it turned me on." I nodded my head to keep from smiling like an idiot. "Thanks Lani, I'm glad you could vibe with them. Sorry for all the sexual pieces it's just," I paused and started at her, "it's something I think about a lot especially in the company of beautiful women." She blushed.

"What do you think about my work?" "It was short, new journal?" She chuckled, "Yes, I left my old one at home." I nodded and continued, "Your imagery is powerful. Each poem is a story and at the end of it I want more and more. Your subject matter is deep and holds my attention. I just have one question," I paused, "about the inspiration behind ", For All The Hoes?"

"If you're asking if I like women, the answer is yes. Far as the poem, it's about my ex-girlfriend. She cheated on me and this was the one piece I wrote about it."

I sat there shocked and processing all the information Lani had just revealed. "You wanna come back to my place to read some of my other work?" She took my silence as a yes and signaled for me to follow her.

The Writers: Part Two

Walking up to Lani's apartment felt like a dream. She was so fucking fine and so fucking thick and she was gay. I just couldn't believe it! I couldn't wait to fuck her. Well I hoped that's why she invited me back to her place.   As we reached the door she grabbed my hand and led me inside. She led me to the couch, putting her hand on my leg. "Danielle, I want to fuck. I haven't been laid in months. Do you think you could help me with that?" I licked my lips, taking her face in my hands, lightly kissing her neck. The fact that I hadn't had pussy in a few weeks added to my aggression. I wanted to take control and have her submit to my wishes.

She moaned in the sweetest way while my tongue found its way to her ear. Gently sucking it, I heard her breaths get slower and deeper. I moved my hand to her breast and rubbed her nipples back and forth becoming more turned on from how they grew behind her shirt. I began to slowly tug her nipples with my teeth, gently then applying increasing pressure. "Harder, she moaned. I felt a growl coming from the back of my throat. I wasn't quite sure what it was about this woman that made me feel so sexually dominant, but I knew I wanted to please her in the worse way. "Bed. Now," I commanded. She got up, I watched her ass sway back and forth and couldn't wait to have her legs in the air while she moaned the greatest pleasure between joy and pain.   I watched as she took

her shirt then pants off. I felt as though she was

dancing for me. She shook her head, allowing

her curls to frame her face. I pressed my body

into hers from behind and slipped my fingers

between her lips. Up and down I rubbed. In and

out of her creases alternating between light

touches and deep kneads. I rubbed the top of her

lips in front of her clit while I sucked her neck.

Her pants told me she liked the current progression. While I knew the moment was solely about fucking. I had the urge to form this intimate connection with her. I took both of my hands on her pussy and slowly pulled her lips apart, then made them come back together. Fast then slow, barely open to gently stretching her lips. I smiled as her essence soaked her panties.

"Please baby," she whimpered. Not yet, I thought. I silently thanked my fantasies for leading me to put on my strap before I left the house (After all, you always had to be prepared for anything). "Get on your knees," I instructed.

I never had the urge before, but there was nothing more I wanted her to do than suck my strap. I lead the head of it to her mouth. She spat on it then took it in slowly, moaning while she looked up at me. I could feel my nipples get so hard they began to hurt. My pussy throbbed like it was being pleased in the best way. "Fuck." I grabbed her head, pushing her down on it further until she tilted her head back as she let me fuck her face. Knowing I was about to cum, she took her fingers under the base of the dildo and rubbed my clit while she sucked it. There was no holding the wave that was about to cum crashing on her. "Lani," I moaned letting the orgasm travel from my pussy to every part of my body. She got up from her knees smiling.

44

"Condom?" She handed my one and bit her lip while I rolled in down the dildo. "Bend over." She slowly poked her ass in the air, I grabbed her hips and rocked slowly then with building intensity until I could hear her pussy dripping as I pounded her. Deep to shallow strokes filled her as I smacked her ass. I loved how she threw it back at me and was determined not to give in again I gave her as much force as I could. I slowly pulled the 7 inch strap out covered in her juices.

"Ride my face." I laid down on the bed anxious to taste her finally. As she lowered herself on my tongue I locked her legs between my elbows ensuring that she couldn't escape. She bounced up and down while I jiggled her ass in my hands. Her sweet cum dripped down my face while she made my tongue please her. I repositioned myself in front of her pussy and covered her with kisses. I slowly kissed up and down her thighs. Sucking the top of her lips like it was her clit. Softly blowing her pleasure center while my fingers explored her tight ass pussy. I felt her gripping my fingers as I fucked her deeper and deeper. I pushed them in until my palm massaged her clit as I stroked her G spot. Fast and slow, slow and fast and finally when I felt her about to explode I stopped. I never wanted her to think this was her doing. It was mine and I would control when she could release.   I sucked her nipples while my fingers stroked her and as I neared my own release I kept hitting her spot until she came down my fingers and dripped all the way to my arm.

Her moan was angelic, powerful and mesmerizing. For the finale, I had one final mission. To taste her ass. I know I know what you're thinking. This is your fist time dealing with this girl there is no way you should be doing that! I knew it too, but the beast was hungry and I needed to feed it.

"Turn around Lani baby." I smacked her backside playfully then started to eat her from behind while I rubbed my own clit. I took her cheeks in my hands and slipped my tongue in the space between her pussy and ass. I spit on it then, let my tongue explore lightly glossing over her tight asshole. Her squirming under me tuned me on even more. I stuck my tongue in her pussy as she backed into me. Begging me to enter her forbidden place. I took my finger to the entrance and slowly parted her. She gasped. As she adjusted herself, I took the opposite finger and put it in her pussy and used them both in synchronous motion to fuck her pussy and ass with deep circular strokes.

Lani went crazy, she started shaking,

dripping, screaming my name. I kissed her left

cheek as I pulled out and collapsed next to her.

My chest heaved as I tried to bring my heartrate

back down. "Let's do that more often," she said

as she leaned over and kissed me. I smiled

knowing we hadn't even begun to explore just

how freaky the other could get.

The Interludes: Part One

Her towel wrapped tight around her body. All I could think about was what was under its contents. In my mind, I was bold and spoke up. Telling her how beautiful she was while I rubbed her shoulders and kissed her neck. Taking the lotion in my hand and massaging from her feet to her inner thighs. In my mind, I was kissing her passionately, deeply, telling her I cared about her. Letting my hands explore her curves. Using my finger to tease her, barely going in and out she moaned. I look her in her eyes, ask if she wants me to stop. She responds by opening her legs wider. I laugh, she's wetter than I imagined. My mouth waters-I push my finger deeper-she calls out my name. "Fuck," I say, as I pull away, surprised by the feeling of my own cum flowing down my legs. I grab her ass and pull her now dripping pussy closer to my mouth. Using my tongue, I take one long lick from the bottom of her lips to the top of her clit, pushing the tip of it deeper as I trace the path back to the bottom of her pussy. I push her left leg up while I vigorously tease her clit with the pointed tip of my tongue. I take a deep breath, inhaling the sweet smell of her.

With my tongue entering her I use my finger in a come here motion and feel her muscles tighten around it. I hear her moans getting louder. knowing she will let go of her orgasm soon. "Cum for me baby," I say as I push my tongue deeper, my face covered in her juices while I push her onto the headboard.

The Interludes: 1.5

You rotate your hips –slowly – on my tongue. Your juices begin to trickle down my cheeks. My tongue relentlessly teases your clit. Taking it into my mouth, sucking on it gently then harder, moving it from side to side then up and down. Your breathing quickens. You moan in ecstasy. I take your hand and guide it towards my throbbing pussy. The heat from your hand on my already sensitive womanhood makes the hairs on the back of my neck stand to attention. In response, I clasped my hands on the top of your hips, forcing you to take every inch of pleasure that my tongue provides as it invades your sweet center. Slow French kisses and deep strokes cause your body to shake. "Shit, "you moan. I whisper "That's my pussy baby." I slide from under you, flip you around, and bury my face in your wetness. Slipping my fingers under your ass I pull you onto my tongue. Your legs clench around my neck as you cum and say "don't stop..."

An Antidote on What I Hate About Being a

Lesbian

Women are at their core emotionally unstable creatures which is why it is the best and also the worst idea to become a lesbian. To ever fall for the touch of another woman, the look in her eyes as she calls you hers; the passion in everything that you do. The good. The bad. The intensifying emotions that turn everything into an overreaction or an underreaction. Secret glimpses of lust and love. As she lays next to you, you think is this just a mistake like the others just a moment to be forgotten like all the others. Is this a glimpse in time to be reflected upon with a smile or is this something more? Something to pay for in eternity or a moment only to be enjoyed? The unsureness of the feeling takes over and I laugh. Turning to the left and right hand out grasping grabbing for someone, anyone to love me half as much as I love them. The pathetic truth steadies itself. Her kiss travels. Your hands wander. Thoughts dominate and moans are expressed. Clothes thrown and flesh scratched. Eyes closes and legs squeezing. Thoughts again If I tell her I miss her will I push her away? You know those lesbian books you read that suck. The only good parts are the sex scenes. And you've had better sex in your fantasies. If I didn't love pussy so much I would give it up. I swear on my own pussy. Well I would if I had two.

Reflections of a Lost Lonely Girl Who Needs to Fuck

I could feel her shaking underneath me. I looked up while her breath caught in her chest and her hand touched my cheek and she whispered "are you sure you are a virgin." I laugh and slip my fingers into her hand. Silence falls over the room while memories travel through your mind taking me to the past.   The first time I saw her she took my breath away. I couldn't help myself but be attracted to her outward beauty. Namely her dreadlocks that cascaded down her back. Next, her smooth brown skin that glowed with no make-up. For the first time since high school my heart skipped a beat. The possibilities and then the insecurities crossed my mind. She could never want me, she probably has a girlfriend anyway, yeah a girlfriend of many years. Well maybe she's single just because everybody thinks she has a girlfriend. But then again maybe I should just introduce myself…I lower my head and smile as I realize she's gone, again. I sigh and wonder if ever my luck with women will improve. I began to give a serious consideration to being straight until I realize no males are on my watch either. Feeling slightly down since I still haven't made the team during cuffing season I decide the next one will really matter and this time being fine won't be enough. A personal deceleration is made and I'm sure that I will be single until the right one comes along. If they ever do. In the middle of my thoughts a hand tapped me on my shoulder. "Excuse me." Beep. Beep. I roll over after my alarm clock wakes me. I groan and realize I was only kissing good morning to my pillow, for the third time this week. "So how did you sleep?" "Good self thanks for asking and thanks for the text too." "Oh you're welcome babe." I stop talking to myself concerned that my suitemates will check on me since they know no one but me is in the room.

I turn on the light, jump out of bed and look in the mirror. I take my hands rub them over my protruding stomach and then think of Mulan, when will my reflection match who I am. I look back at myself and think how can I encourage others when I'm so unsure of things myself. The thought crosses my mind that this isn't about me anymore. Bible study crosses my mind "It's no way you can be a homosexual and gratify your flesh and love God at the same time." Closing my eyes I imagine a future where people don't pit differences against each other, where people don't put extreme limits on religion. With my eyes still closed I whisper a prayer God please help all of my gay brothers and sisters. Amen. Eyes still closed I feel oddly at peace and smile.

Glance in the mirror and give myself a

compliment you're kind of cute girl I say with a

smile. Another day, another glance. Walking

around campus I always wonder if girls can read

my mind. I promise looking into some women's

mind I think they can see the pure list

protruding from my eyes. I think if only they

had known how long it had been since I

experienced the touch of a woman, a man, a dog,

anybody at that matter then they would

understand. My desire for a companion wasn't

simply physical or a want it was a spiritual need.

My thoughts travel to all the fine ass studs I

have seen around campus. Then I ask myself

why haven't I approached them. The old,

vintage me would have approached any stud

within three feet of me with no hesitation at all.
One rejection only leading closer to the actual
one. But 20 months after the break up with my
failed first love and a seemingly dormant libido I
seemed to have subconsciously put a barrier
between myself and all women. Despite the
potential of finding love I just couldn't seem to
find a reason to put myself out there again. I was
too afraid to get my heartbroken again. Too
afraid to risk giving myself to someone who
couldn't give themselves back to me.

So I watched and observed and smiled when others got into fabulous relationships around me. I laughed at all of the new lesbian team members and I stayed to myself. I focused on school, workouts, and church. I made getting a six pack my obsession and limited late night fantasies to once a month. I was content and happy. And only a tad lonely when my period came and I realized I had no girlfriend to warm lotion between her hands while she applied pressure to my lower back, slowly kiss my neck, and stop to bring me some Midol. Instead I kept random journals filled with notes that sometimes went together and sometimes didn't. My most recent page was somewhere between Black consciousness and sensuality.

It is impossible to separate yourself from ur writing either it was u in the past, u in the present or some written down fantssdy of who u want to become

- It seems that white people have always been amazed

and obsessed by the things black people could do that they couldn't .

- dreadhead chronicles, comedy. Sketch. Short.

I have to see my parts
Lint equals fear
Parts
Lint
Parts again

Untitled

Part I.

Elevation.

Levitations Glance in my eyes

Imagining Visions of you naked.

Part II

Vibrations.

Sensations.

Lost in pleasure- the moans run together

Voice in vibrato, moans are the motto.

By the time I finished the page. I felt
overwhelmed. I stopped and realized I was
always like this when I felt alone. What else
could I do, but write when loneliness took over. I
took a deep breath and realized I needed to stop
all this thinking about deep shit and admit the
truth I needed to fuck!

The Interludes 2.0: The Encounter

My eyes painstakingly sought her presence and when they found her they raked over her body slowly, not knowing when they would have another opportunity to share the elixir she breathed. Attempting to be discreet, I shuffled along only to encounter the pill of a magnet. I could feel my cheeks flush as my eyes rose to meet her face.   Cymbals clanked in the stars confirming this meeting as fate. Her eyes deep as a coal pit, seared into me causing a fire to ignite within my chest. Seconds gave way to an eternity as cool fire which started at my heart began to spread throughout my body making its way to every organ, touching every limb. Time continued. I felt guilty now and angry at myself for being diaphanous yet again.

I cursed myself for falling prey to her beauty-yet again.

My school day dragged along until it was suddenly over. Most of the students had left long ago so with no signs of human life present I allowed my thoughts to excavate the inner cage of my mind. I began to ask myself rhetorical questions like I wonder how it feels to...The sound of heels tapping against linoleum disrupted my thoughts. I was no longer alone. Could it be her?

I wiped my hands on my pants as I felt the nervousness building in my atmosphere. *Click. Click. Click.* The volume of the clicking increased. Whoever it was continued to get closer. Like a magnet I felt her eyes drawing mine towards hers.

There she was, no more than 5 feet away from my touch. I saw it before it happened, her shoe slipped on the glossy floors, her arm reached out for the wall that was out of her grasp. Her arms waved, trying to regain a balance she knew was lost. She was falling like the first mist of autumn, but before the sun could evaporate her presence, I caught her.

She looked up, her gaze piercing the deepest parts of my spirit. I could feel her heart beating steady like the flow of the Nile while mine was rumbling like the beat of a million drums. In her arms she felt vulnerable-real. My eyes traveled across her body noting the protrusion of her nipples though her dress.

My eyes lingered, savoring the taste of her pussy with my imagination. I knew we were outlasting the moment. I had to let go. After I helped her regain her balance she straightened her dress. "Thank you." "You're welcome." We walked our separate ways.

Shakin'

I wanted to fuck her. The thought struck me at first as appalling. At first I had only seen her as a friend. I don't know if it was my hormones or the chilllness of the day. All I know is suddenly I had the desire to be lost in her pussy with her legs around my neck pushing my tongue deeper in her, feeling her legs shake while she called out my name. I needed to please her. I needed to feel her up against me. It had been so long…"Dee." "Huh?" I shook my head and my leg pulling myself out of my incomplete fantasy. I looked up at her dress, saw the way it was hugging her curves and immediately thought about… "Dee, are you going to open the door for me or just stand there?" "My bad Gina. I uh just was thinking about something." "You musta got some good pussy last night" she joked. "Girl

stop playing," I replied. "You know nobody

wants me." I smirked and we both laughed.

Since my fitness transformation, dropping 120

pounds and training as an amateur body builder

the amount of girls interested in me had

exponentially increased. The fact that I had

black and gold dreads flowing down my back

only added to my sex appeal. I wasn't a stud and

I wasn't a fem. I usually found myself dressing

somewhat in the middle, neither too masculine

nor feminine. I refused to be label a stem and

would argue with people that I was not part of a

flower. I preferred the term no label. Dressing in

the middle got me attention from girls who

weren't ready to accept their lesbian status and

studs who didn't like dealing with fem's drama.

I was lowkey, confident, and enjoying myself. I

hadn't been in a serious relationship ever and

getting pussy wasn't on my list of priorities, but

I got more than enough to keep me satisfied.

"Gina," I leaned over and whispered to her.

"What?" "You look damn good in that dress girl." She hit me on the arm. "Dee, if you don't stop playing with me." "I'm not playing," I said. "I wanna fuck you." She looked over at me. The seconds passed and I watched her lick her lips. "Tell me what you want to do." "Sit back it's a movie," I said and smiled. I texted her my response. "I'm going to make your body beg for me. I'm going to eat your pussy so passionately that you think my tongue is the missing piece to your pussy. All the times you told me about the niggas that couldn't fuck you right. I took notes. I know what you like. I'm going to fuck you so good that when I leave you reach for me in the middle of the night and text my phone to come over." I watched her read it. For a few minutes we sat in silence watching the movie when she grabbed my hand and slid it up her thigh. I could feel the heat coming from her. I looked over and saw her eyes closed and her head titled back. I knew she had been wet from the moment I told her she looked good. I wanted her but not like this. I had made up in my mind I was going to tease her until she and I couldn't take it. I just hope I had the discipline to get through my plan.

As she slid my hand up towards her panties I felt her take her hand away as if she were content to let me finish the job. I slowly took my hand and rubbed my palm over her wet pussy, felt it throbbing and went around in circle around her lips until her panties were soaked. "Shit, "she moaned. That was my signal to stop and pull my hand away. I smiled knowing I had her dripping before I even put a finger in her. I knew this was going to be an enjoyable night. She looked over at me with a face that said why the hell did you stop. I texted her "wait." The next time I looked over I saw her with her hand under her dress and her eyes closed. I pulled her arm away from her and took her fingers from her legs. One by one I licked them from top to bottom. Then I took her hand and placed it on my lap while I un-buttoned my jeans. I took a chance and lead her fingers to my boxers. Then I whispered to her. "You just couldn't wait could you?" I reached in my boxers and pulled out my strap. She looked down and smiled then she got on her knees and put it in her mouth. The whole time she was sucking it she was looking up at me turning me on. I bit my lip trying not to moan. When I could feel myself about to climax I said "Stop Gina. We can finish this later." She pouted but got up. The first round was even.

The walk back to the car was filled with sexual tension. The ride back to her house was silent. Soon as she closed the door I walked over to her and started kissing her lips her neck, rubbing on her ass as I pressed her against the door. I slipped my shirt over my head while she took her dress off. I undid her bra and as her nipples fell to my face I took one in my mouth and gently sucked it while I felt her grinding her pelvis into me. I got excited and started tugging on her nipples with my teeth . "Fuck." I rubbed her other nipple between my thumb and finger feeling it get harder and slightly pinched it. She moaned in pleasure mixed with the slightest pain. I took my finger and slipped it in her panties to feel how wet she was. Her pussy juices covered my finger while I rubbed it across her clit up and down her lips then in and out of her hole. She was so tight that I could only press the tip of my finger. I stepped away from the wall and said," Where is your bedroom."

We walked into the bedroom. I told her to lay down on the bed. As she laid down I got on top of her and started sucking on her neck while I rubbed her nipples and kissed my way down her stomach to her steaming pussy. I kissed it like I needed its flavor to stay alive. Up one lip and down the other I covered her pussy in soft, slow, sensual kisses while she grinded her pelvis upward in anticipation of my tongue. I lifted her legs and pushed my tongue deep in her warm hole so effortlessly she didn't realize it. The higher I pushed her legs the more she pushed my head down, pulling my dreads, and saying "Shit Dee." She came on my face but it didn't stop my tongue from going in and out of her sweetness quickly at first then licking up to her clit and taking it into my warm mouth. While my tongue did its magic I pushed two fingers deep in her pussy like they were a dick. She started to shake beneath me. As I felt her muscles tightening I told her to relax for me. I grabbed her ass and massaged it while my fingers invaded her pussy. She started to squirt. "Shitttt," she moaned. I knew she had cum a few times without me stopping, but I hadn't cum yet, I had to make this a fuck she would never forget. I got under her put her pussy over my mouth and held onto her thighs while she fucked my face. I felt her warm juices covering my face and as she came she rolled off my face. I opened her legs and slid the strap in, kissing her as inch by inch I got lost in her pussy. "Fuck me Dee." I could feel the pressure growing between my legs while I increased her pleasure. I fucked her fast then slow with half the shaft followed by deep strokes and as I came I pulled out and said "shit." I grabbed her ass in my hand and slid my finger in from the back. Feeling how easily my fingers slid in and out of her wetness I knew she was completely relaxed with me. I pushed in another finger and felt her muscles tighten around them while I kissed her deeply pushing her back into the bed while my fingers fucked her. I thought it would be good, but not like this I thought as she moaned out my name. "Umm," I said as I put her down and tied to catch my breath.

I wasn't ready for what happened next. She climbed on top of me and started kissing my neck with soft, gentle kisses. She knew she had me right where she wanted me as I had told her countless times that my neck made me lose my sense of reality. She made her way down from my neck to my breast, around my nipples, biting them just a bit, just how I like. Sensual kisses made their way down my abs, over my thighs. She reached under me and slid the strap off while she started kissing my pussy. She had just started but, I already was squirming. I was used to giving, not receiving and the pleasure that was rippling through my body, starting at my stomach and cascading through my whole body was almost unbearable. She kissed up and down my lips until she made her way to my clit. When she started humming on it I knew she had seen one too many lesbian pornos. "Fuck Gina," I said in a voice so high I didn't recognize it as mine. "Oh my God, Stop," I moaned. "Only if you come for me," she replied in the sultriest voice. She took her first finger and rubbed it around my clit and used her tongue to tease my hole. "Shit" I moaned as I let go of the orgasm I was holding. When she got up smiling and said "I think I win." I knew we had many more rounds to play...

Random Poems to my Lover

Sometimes I think about you and write you poems.

Face Time
What a surprise
Who knew
Looking in your eyes
Was all it takes to be
Completely mesmerized. Blinded by
Visions of diving between your thighs
With no compromise
Driven by your moans
And the higher octave tone.
Got damn
Let me act like I'm looking at my phone
Feel the lust calling
It's been way too long.
Panties dripping
And I didn't even touch
Just looking into your eyes it's more than
enough.

Intermission
Breath quickens
I feel the rush,
Lost in your brown skin
No comparing it even to all the places I been.
I'm hungry now
Want only your p*ssy for din
So I can tease you then stick my juicy tongue all
the way in.

Unspoken
Heart throbbing to the beat
Matching the clitensity,
Or the power of this energy
Between you and me.
Couldn't concentrate if I wanted
Too focused on the moment -
Making you feel it
When you know we both need it.
Don't want to just fuck you
But the experience of the experience.
So wet right now
The shit got me delirious
Thinking about you playing with it got me
serious
Taking notes in my head so I can
Make the water fall from your pyramid.
Your body grinding on mine in this bed
Lift your leg up higher
Lose your fingers in my dreads.
Damn
Fuck this sheets
Bust that nut just for me.
Don't mean to be vulgar
 But,
When the instincts take over
Tell me what you need
 I *Ache* just to please
And Fulfill the wildest fantasy of your dreams.

But For now,
Keep drippin'
 down my chin
cause
We just getting started
and it's nowhere near the end.

Unplanned Surprise

The smell of her made my breath quicken with such an intensity that I could feel my heart pounding against my chest. Her moans of "fuck me baby" motivated me, made my hips thrust into her wetness deeper and harder. I grabbed her hips bringer them closer to mine, while I pulled the strap out slowly and slid it back into her. She responded with passionate grunts. I felt my own orgasm building behind my clit, throbbing, screaming to be released. But, I clenched my inner thighs tighter together. I couldn't succumb to my own orgasm. Not yet anyways. I promised myself she would cum at least 3 times to my one and my ego wouldn't let me answer the call of pleasure.

I bit her shoulder frustrated I couldn't feel her wetness around me, but satisfied that I could feel her essence dripping onto my thighs. I reached around and covered her nipples with my hands cupping them between my fingers while I slowly ground my hands into her waist. The sound of her pants were louder than the music in the background-Silk's "A Meeting in my Bedroom." I moaned with her, unable to control my animalistic nature. I felt the need to dominate her body, to control the strength of her orgasm all the while preventing my own. My aggression rose the harder I felt my clit get and as I felt the juices escaping my own lips I pushed her hips further down then reached around and grabbed her hair. My hands tightened around her neck, then softened to bring her body up from the bed. I turned her around, made her face me, and pushed her against the wall supporting the bed.

"Open your eyes, "I commanded with a voice I didn't even recognize as my own. I lifted her legs around my waist and put my arms on the wall on both sides of her. I nuzzled my lips against her neck while nibbling on her ear. "Tell me how you need to be fucked, " I said as I felt her nails dig into my back. "Slower, "she responded. I reacted by picking her up and laying her on the bed, ass down, pussy up. As I laid her on the bed our lips met passionately, her tongue tugging mine towards hers and me submitting to her pull. She led the kiss, I followed, while she began to suck on my bottom lip I moaned. We flipped positions, now with her on top, while I laid on my back.

Her lips traveled lower covering my chest with soft kisses and passionate caresses. I could feel my already hard nipples getting tighter in response to her chest against mine. She slipped my nipple in her mouth swirling it around her mouth quicker as my breaths increased. Her other hand found its way to the opposite one and squeezed it forcefully. "Fuck," I breathlessly stated. Comfortable in her now found position she sent jolts of shock through my body as she lightly bit my erect nipples. A distinct moan escaped my lips as I let go of the orgasm that had been building since I entered the room.

"Is that for me baby," she laughed as she slipped her hand under the underwear hold the plastic toy in place. "Umm," I moaned rising my hips up to meet the probing of her fingers. I closed my eyes, taking in the feeling of the sexual energy that flowed between us. I bit my lip, determined not to moan again while her fingers gently rubbed the outside of my pussy, dipped around my clit in small circles with slowly increasing pressure and back again. My legs opened wider, inviting her deeper into my essence. I felt my juices covering her fingers and a slow throb building behind my clit. I knew I was going to explode, but not yet.

I grabbed her hand and brought it to my face. Looking into her eyes, I took her finger into my mouth twirling my tongue gently up and down the shaft of her fingers until there was no more of me left to taste. "Ride me," I instructed. As she lowered herself down onto me I grabbed her hips, rocking them gently back and forth until we found a rhythm together. And in that moment of ecstasy, with her breast bouncing and our hands intertwined, with both of our orgasms reaching the point of overflow, it felt like our souls were touching.

She switched positions until she laid next to me. I felt the residue of her climax on my thighs and I leaned over and kissed her. "I hope you didn't think we were finished," I whispered, as I kissed her lips after all I had a point to prove.

Pussy.

If there was one thing I could never get enough of it was pussy. I loved to think about it, I loved to touch it, to watch it. Hell, I even loved saying it as it was phonetically pleasing. I loved the way the "u" stretched out from the "p" the way the double "s" ensured all of the syllables were stated. For someone who loves pussy, there was nothing like having the desire for pussy go unfilled.   It had been well over a month since I had seen her. I was struggling to keep the memories of the last time we fucked alive. I tried to think about it once during the day and twice at night so I could remember the details. Hear her moans. Feel her nails grazing my back as I sank deeper into her love. Smell how wet she got for me. Still every day the details faded more and more. Until all I could so was fantasize about the next opportunity to make love. Another morning and all I could think about was substituting my hot coffee for her warm juices gliding across my tongue. I sighed. I decided to send my love a nice long text e-mail message with specific instructions.

Take a shower, Rub your body down with lotion SLOWLY, Remain naked and Facetime me. Next grab three things: ice and vibrator.

1. Grab an ice cube and let it melt a little in your hands, then drag it across your left then right nibble, repeat in smaller then bigger circles until it melts. Then grab your nipple and gently pinch it, hold for one complete breath then release slowly, repeat.

2. When ready get another ice cube and rub it up and down your stomach STOP when you get to the top of your pussy. Rub the ice in the area between your thighs and your pussy then down to your clit.

3. Use one hand to feel your clit, use the other to pull your lips back. Get another ice cube and rub it around your clit then slide it up and down. Now, use the ice to circle your clit slowly.

4. Get another ice cube and slide it between your lips, increase the speed and rock your hips into it,

5. Now get your vibrator, rub it up and down your clit and with each rub say " this tight, wet, pretty pink pussy belongs to you juicy and only you.

As you fuck yourself, think of the ice as my

tongue, close your eyes and feel me breathing on

your pussy, licking it slowly, then faster, until

it's just how you like it. Feel me picking up your

legs and wrapping them around my shoulders

as I slide my fingers into you deep then deeper

and I stroke your pussy gently then gentler until

I find your spot and fuck you until...I think

you've had enough. I closed my computer and

checked my phone.

I checked my calendar the countdown for the next trip was three months away. "Fuck," I slowly said. I weighed the options in my mind, I could go home and have a quick masturbation session or attempt a video chat over a fuzzy internet connection. Walking home I decided to check my flight rewards, maybe I could have a free trip in the works. As luck would have it, I had enough points to pay for 80 percent of a round trip ticket. I raced home packing my bag and headed to the airport.   Three hours later I reached my destination. I had arranged for my love to pick me up from the airport. Little did she know this trip was for a very specific purpose-a weekend of nonstop fucking. I stopped by the restroom to check my pants making sure the strap was not protruding and checked my pocket for a condom. I left smiling about what was about to happen.   When I saw her pull up my clit jumped. I felt my nipples tighten around my nipple rings. My breath quickened. I opened the car door slowly. "Hey baby, you look beautiful." I stopped for a second to admire her beauty. Clear brown skin with deep brown eyes and natural hair with curves in all the right places. I smiled overtaken by her natural beauty. "Thanks, how was the trip." I tried to pay attention to the small talk but all I could think about was my face between her legs in the backseat of the car. "Pull over," I instructed. She stopped on a dimly lit street before the highway began. "Backseat now." She slid into the backseat, I followed closely behind and slid my pants down. Our lips touched, the air was full of lust and passion I tugged at her lips, wrapped them around my own. Kissed her so deeply that she moaned. I lightly kissed her neck and slid my hand under her dress. No panties. I looked up at her, she laughed "I know what this weekend is about." I laughed slid the condoms over my fingers and lifted her leg for easier access.   To say that she was wet would have been an understatement. My fingers slid into her soaking pussy effortlessly. She pushed herself against my hand with my palm rubbing her clit with every stroke. "Shit baby." I moaned knowing I was about to cum feeling my own wetness drip down my leg. She fucked my fingers faster and faster bucking against them as I twisted them toward her G spot. I felt her pussy tightening and slowly slid my fingers out of her dripping pussy.   I slid the condom over the 7-inch strap and entered her slowly. While I fucked her I looked her in the eyes. Felt the animalistic passion take over and began to fuck her faster. I wrapped her legs around me. Sweat dripped down my forehead the faster I pumped. "You like that shit baby," I moaned. "Yes baby," she moaned in response. I took the strap out rubbed it on her clit then slid it in slowly inch by inch. I loved watching her take the strap. I knew my own orgasm was close.

"Ride me." We shifted positions, her ass facing me as she sat on the strap. "Damn," I exhaled. As she lowered herself, I thrusted my hips up faster than she expected. "Fuck, she exclaimed. I put my thumb over her ass while she fucked me. Feeling how wet she was and the pressure of her on my clit I finally came all over the backseat. I rubbed her clit until she exclaimed "Shit baby I can't take anymore." I helped her slide off me. We both sat there absorbed in the thoughts of letting lust completely take over. She laid her head on my shoulder. "I've been wanting to do that for a while." "Don't worry, we've got all weekend," I responded as I kissed her forehead.

About the Author:

Khalani Jones is somewhere in the world creating, living, learning and constantly evolving. And striving every day to live in her truth and encourages others to do the same. She wants you to know that all stories will be continued in Part Two.

www.ingramcontent.com/pod-product-compliance
Lightning Source LLC
Chambersburg PA
CBHW060057150626
46556CB00017BA/1736